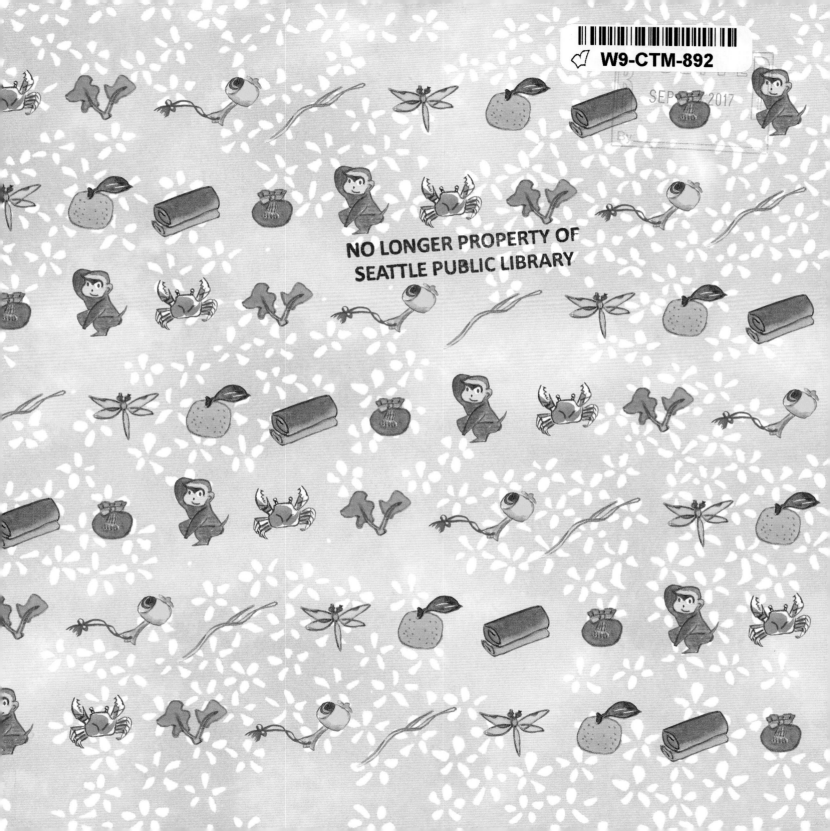

Published by Tuttle Publishing, an imprint of Periplus Editions (HK) Ltd

Library of Congress Cataloging-in-Publication Data

Sakade, Florence.
   Little One-Inch and other Japanese children's favorite stories / compiled by Florence Sakade; illustrated by Yoshisuke Kurosaki. — 1st ed.
      51 p. : col. ill. ; 24 cm.
   Summary: A collection of traditional Japanese folktales, including "Little One-Inch," "The Spider Weaver," and "The Crab and the Monkey."
   ISBN 978-4-8053-0995-7 (hardcover)
1. Tales—Japan. [1. Folklore—Japan.] I. Kurosaki, Yoshisuke, 1905– ill. II. Title.
   PZ8.1.S2155Li 2008
   [398.20952]—dc22

                                    2007052087

ISBN 978-4-8053-0995-7

Distributed by:

North America, Latin America & Europe
Tuttle Publishing
364 Innovation Drive
North Clarendon, VT 05759-9436
U.S.A.
Tel: 1 (802) 773-8930;
Fax: 1 (802) 773-6993
info@tuttlepublishing.com
www.tuttlepublishing.com

Japan
Tuttle Publishing
Yaekari Building, 3rd Floor
5-4-12 Osaki, Shinagawa-ku,
Tokyo 141 0032
Tel: (81) 3 5437-0171
Fax: (81) 3 5437-0755
sales@tuttle.co.jp
www.tuttle.co.jp

Asia Pacific
Berkeley Books Pte. Ltd.
61 Tai Seng Avenue #02-12
Singapore 534167
Tel: (65) 6280-1330
Fax: (65) 6280-6290
inquiries@periplus.com.sg
www.periplus.com

First edition
17 16 15 14
10 9 8 7 6 5 4 3 2

Printed in Malaysia   1203TW

TUTTLE PUBLISHING® is a registered trademark of Tuttle Publishing, a division of Periplus Editions (HK) Ltd.

The Tuttle Story: "Books to Span the East and West"

Many people are surprised to learn that the world's leading publisher of books on Asia had humble beginnings in the tiny American state of Vermont. The company's founder, Charles E. Tuttle, belonged to a New England family steeped in publishing.

Immediately after WWII, Tuttle served in Tokyo under General Douglas MacArthur and was tasked with reviving the Japanese publishing industry. He later founded the Charles E. Tuttle Publishing Company, which thrives today as one of the world's leading independent publishers.

Though a westerner, Tuttle was hugely instrumental in bringing a knowledge of Japan and Asia to a world hungry for information about the East. By the time of his death in 1993, Tuttle had published over 6,000 books on Asian culture, history and art—a legacy honored by the Japanese emperor with the "Order of the Sacred Treasure," the highest tribute Japan can bestow upon a non-Japanese.

With a backlist of 1,500 titles, Tuttle Publishing is more active today than at any time in its past—inspired by Charles Tuttle's core mission to publish fine books to span the East and West and provide a greater understanding of each.

Little One-Inch

And Other Japanese Children's Favorite Stories

Compiled by Florence Sakade

Illustrated by Yoshisuke Kurosaki

TUTTLE PUBLISHING
Tokyo • Rutland, Vermont • Singapore

Contents

Publisher's Foreword

In today's ever-shrinking world—where e-mails zoom from one continent to another in the space of a heartbeat, where travelers can easily pass through political boundaries once more solid than stone—understanding and tolerance have never been at a higher premium. Parents and teachers are increasingly aware of the need for children to be citizens of this small world who will grow into thinking adults who, while proud of their own traditions and heritage, respect the varied experiences and viewpoints to be found in other cultures.

This collection of traditional stories can help set children on this enlightened path, introducing them to marvelous characters and places that have been loved by Japanese children for centuries.

Each of these stories—amusing, instructive and wise—is to be found in many forms and versions in Japan, and often in other countries as well. We have tried to select the most interesting version in each case and, in our translations, to remain true to the spirit of the Japanese originals. At the same time we have explained in the stories customs and situations that Western readers might not understand.

These timeless stories have both united and delighted children for hundreds of years, and will continue to do so for countless generations to come.

The Spider Weaver

Long ago there was a young farmer named Yosaku. One day he was working in the fields and saw a snake about to eat a spider. Yosaku felt sorry for the spider, so he ran at the snake with his hoe and drove it away.

The spider disappeared into the grass, but first it seemed to pause a moment and bow in thanks toward Yosaku.

One morning not long after that, Yosaku was in his house when he heard a tiny voice outside calling, "Yosaku, Yosaku!" He opened the door and saw a beautiful girl standing there.

"I heard that you are looking for someone to weave cloth for you," said the girl. "Won't you please let me live here and weave for you?"

Yosaku was very pleased because he did need someone to help him. He showed the girl the weaving room and she started to work at the loom with cotton. At the end of the day Yosaku went to see what she had done, and was very surprised to find that she had woven eight long pieces of cloth, enough to make eight kimono. He had never known anyone could weave so much in a single day.

"How ever did you weave so much cloth?" he asked the girl.

But instead of answering him, she said, "You mustn't ask me that. And you must never come into the weaving room while I am at work."

But Yosaku was very curious. So one day he slipped quietly to the weaving room and peeped in the window. What he saw really surprised him! It was not the girl who was seated at the loom, but a large spider, weaving very fast with its eight legs, and for thread it was using its own spider web, which came out of its mouth.

Yosaku looked again and saw that it was the same spider that he had saved from the snake. Then he understood. The spider had been so thankful that it had wanted to do something to help him. So it had turned itself into a beautiful girl to help him weave cloth. By eating the cotton that was in the weaving room, it could spin it into thread and weave it into cloth very, very quickly.

Yosaku was very grateful for the spider's help. He saw that the cotton was almost used up, so the next morning he set out for the nearest

village, on the other side of the mountains, to buy some more. He bought a big bundle of cotton and started home, carrying it on his back.

Along the way a terrible thing happened. As Yosaku sat down to rest, the same snake that he'd driven away from the spider came and slipped inside the bundle of cotton. But Yosaku didn't know about this. So he carried the cotton home and gave it to the girl.

She was very glad to get the cotton, because she had now used up all the cotton that was left. So she took it and went to the weaving room.

As soon as the girl was inside the weaving room she turned back into a spider and began eating the cotton so that she could spin it into thread. The spider ate and ate and ate, and then suddenly, when it had eaten down to the bottom of the bundle—the snake jumped right out of the cotton and straight at her!

The snake opened its mouth wide to swallow the spider. The spider was very frightened and jumped out the window, but the snake went wriggling after it. But the spider had eaten so much cotton that it couldn't run fast, and the snake soon caught up with it. Again the snake opened its mouth wide to gulp the spider down. But just then a wonderful thing happened.

Old Man Sun, up in the sky, had been watching what was happening. He knew how kind the spider had been to Yosaku and he felt very sorry for the poor little spider. So he reached down with a sunbeam and caught hold of the end of the web that was sticking out of the spider's mouth, and he gently lifted the spider high up into the sky, where the snake couldn't reach her.

The spider was very grateful to Old Man Sun for saving her from the snake. And so she used all the cotton inside her body to weave many beautiful, fleecy clouds high up in the sky.

This is the reason, they say, why clouds are soft and white like cotton, and also why a spider and a cloud are both called by the same name in Japan—kumo.

Little One-Inch

There was once a kindly couple who had no children. One day they went to a shrine and prayed for a baby, saying, "Oh, please give us a child. We want a child very badly."

On their way home from the shrine, they heard a tiny crying sound coming from a patch of grass. They looked in the grass, and there they found a tiny little baby boy, wrapped in a bright red blanket. "This child has come in answer to our prayers," they said. So they took the little baby home with them and raised him as their son.

Now this baby was so tiny that he wasn't as large as your thumb, and even as he grew older he stayed the same size. He was just about an inch tall, so the couple named him Little One-Inch.

One day, when he had grown older, Little One-Inch said to his mother and father, "Thank you very much for raising me so well. But now I must go out into the world and make my fortune."

The couple tried to keep him from leaving, saying he was too tiny to go out into the world. But Little One-Inch insisted, so finally they said, "All right, we'll help you get ready." And they gave him a needle to use for a sword, a rice bowl to use for a boat, and a chopstick to use for an oar.

Little One-Inch got in his boat and waved goodbye to his parents, promising to return home when he had made his fortune. Then he went floating down the river in his rice bowl boat, paddling with his chopstick.

Little One-Inch had floated along for many, many leagues when a frog accidentally knocked into his boat and turned it over. Little One-Inch was a very good swimmer and he swam to the riverbank, where he found himself standing before a great lord's house.

Little One-Inch looked at the house and saw that it must belong to a very wealthy lord. He walked boldly up to the front door and called out. A servant came to the door, but he couldn't see anyone.

"Here I am, down here!" cried Little One-Inch. "Look down here!"

The servant looked down at the ground. At first all he could see was a pair of wooden sandals that his lord used when he went out walking. Then the servant looked closer and saw the tiny figure of Little One-Inch standing beside the sandals. He was so surprised that he hurried off to tell his lord.

The lord came to the front door himself and looked down at Little One-Inch standing there proudly, his needle-sword at his hip. "Why, hello there, little warrior," he said. "What do you want here?"

"I've come out into the world to seek my fortune," said Little One-Inch. "And if you'll have me, let me become one of your guards. I may be small, but I can fight very well with this fine sword."

The lord was very amused to hear the tiny boy speak such bold words. "All right," he said, "you can come and be a playmate for my daughter, the princess."

So Little One-Inch became the companion of the princess. They soon became good friends, reading and playing together every day. The princess even made a bed for Little One-Inch in her jewel box.

One day Little One-Inch and the princess went to visit a temple near the lord's house. Suddenly, a terrible green devil appeared, carrying a magic hammer. When the devil saw the princess he ran towards her to carry her off.

Little One-Inch quickly drew his needle-sword and began sticking the green devil's toes with it. But the devil's skin was so thick that the tiny sword couldn't go through it. As the devil got closer to the princess, Little One-Inch climbed up the devil's body and out onto his arm. Then he waved his sword at the devil's nose. This made the devil so angry that he opened his mouth wide to let out a roar.

At that moment Little One-Inch gave a big leap and jumped right onto the green devil's face and began poking his nose with the sword. Now the devil's nose was very tender and the needle hurt very much. He was so surprised that he jumped up, yelled and went running away. He even dropped his magic hammer.

The princess said, "Thank you, Little One-Inch," and picked up the magic hammer. "Now we can use this to make a wish!" She shook the hammer in the air and said, "Please let Little One-Inch grow taller!"

Sure enough, each time she shook the hammer, Little One-Inch grew one inch taller. The princess kept shaking it until he was just as tall as she was. They were both very happy, and the lord was very grateful when he heard what Little One-Inch had done.

When they were a few years older, Little One-Inch and the princess were married, and they lived very happily ever after.

The Badger and the Magic Fan

In Japan, goblins are called tengu and they all have very long noses. Now once upon a time three little tengu children were playing in the forest. They had a magic fan with them, and when they fanned their noses with one side of the fan, their noses would grow longer and longer, and when they fanned their noses with the other side, their noses would shrink back to their original sizes.

The three tengu children were having a wonderful time fanning their noses. But just then a badger came by and saw what they were doing. "My! How I'd like to have a fan like that!" he said to himself. And then he thought of a good trick. Badgers are always playing tricks and can change themselves into any shape they want. So the badger changed himself into a little girl. He took four bean-jam buns with him and went to the tengu children.

"Hello, children," said the badger. "I've brought you some wonderful bean-jam buns. Please let me play with you!"

The tengu children were delighted because they loved to eat bean-jam buns. But there were four delicious buns to be divided among the three of them, and they immediately started arguing over who would get the very last bun.

Finally the badger said, "I know how to decide who gets the last bun. Close your eyes, and the one who can keep his eyes closed and hold his breath the longest will win the last bun."

The tengu children all agreed. The badger counted, "One! Two! Three!" and they closed their eyes hard. As soon as they did, the badger grabbed the magic fan and went running away with it as fast as he could, leaving the tengu children in the forest with their eyes closed and still holding their breath.

"Ha, ha, ha!" laughed the badger. "I certainly made fools out of those tengu children!" he said, and went walking along his way.

Soon the badger came to a temple. There he saw a beautiful girl dressed in very expensive clothes. He felt sure she was the daughter of a wealthy man, and in fact her father was a great lord and the richest man in all of Japan. So the badger crept up quietly behind her on tiptoe. Quick as a flash he fanned her nose with the magic fan. Instantly her nose grew a yard long!

What a terrible to-do there was! Here was the beautiful little rich girl with the nose a yard long! Her father called all the doctors in the land, but none of them could do anything to make her nose shorter. He spent a lot of money on medicines, but nothing did any good. Finally in desperation he said, "I'll give my daughter as a wife and half my fortune to anyone who can make her nose grow short again!"

When the badger heard this, he said, "That's what I've been waiting for." He quickly went to the great lord and announced that he had come to fix her nose. So the great lord took the badger to his daughter's room. The badger took out the magic fan and fanned her nose with the other side of it. In the twinkling of an eye her nose was short again!

The great lord was very happy and started making preparations for the wedding. The badger was very happy too because not only was he going to get a beautiful wife, he was also going to get a large fortune.

On the day of the wedding, the badger was so happy that he ate and drank too much and became very hot and sleepy. Without thinking, he lay back on some pillows, closed his eyes and began fanning himself with the magic fan. Instantly his nose began to grow longer. But as he was half asleep, he didn't know this was happening. So he kept fanning and fanning himself and his nose kept on growing and growing. It went right through the ceiling and high into the sky until it pierced the clouds.

Now, above the clouds some heavenly workers were building a bridge across the Milky Way. "Look at that!" they cried, pointing to the badger's nose. "That pole's just the right size for our bridge. Come on, let's pull it up!"

And they began pulling on the badger's nose. How this surprised the badger! He started out of his sleep, crying, "Ouch! Help, help!" And he began to fan his nose with the other side of the fan as fast as he possibly could.

But it was much too late. The heavenly workers kept on pulling, crying, "Heave, ho!" until they had pulled the badger into the sky, and no one ever saw him again.

Mr. Lucky Straw

Once upon a time, long ago, there was a good-hearted young man named Shobei who lived in a village in Japan.

One day on his way home from working in the fields, Shobei fell down the steps that led to his village and tumbled over and over on the ground. When he finally stopped tumbling, Shobei discovered that he had caught a piece of straw in his hand.

"Well, well," he said, "a piece of straw is a worthless thing, but it seems I was meant to pick this one up, so I won't throw it away."

As Shobei went walking along, holding the straw in his hand, a dragonfly came flying in circles around his head. "What a pest!" he said. "I'll show this dragonfly not to bother me!" And he caught the dragonfly and tied the straw around its tail.

Shobei went on walking, holding on to the dragonfly, and presently met a woman walking with her son. When the little boy saw the dragonfly, he wanted it very badly. "Mother, I want that dragonfly," he said. "Please, please, please!"

"Here you are, little boy, you can have my dragonfly!" said Shobei, handing the boy the straw. To thank Shobei, the little boy's mother gave him three oranges. Shobei thanked her and went on his way.

Before long, Shobei met a peddler resting by the road. The peddler was so thirsty that he was about to faint. There were no streams nearby and Shobei felt very sorry for the peddler, so he gave him the three oranges so that he could drink the juice.

The peddler was very grateful, and in exchange he gave Shobei three pieces of cloth that he was carrying to market. Shobei thanked him and went on his way.

As Shobei was walking along, he came across a fine carriage with many attendants. The carriage belonged to a princess who was on her way to town. The princess just happened to look out of the carriage and saw the beautiful pieces of cloth that Shobei was carrying. She said, "Oh, what pretty pieces of cloth you have there. Please let me have them." Shobei gave the princess the three pieces of cloth, and to thank him, she gave him a large bag of coins.

Shobei took the coins and bought many fields with them. Then he divided the fields among the people of his village. Thus everyone had his or her own piece of land, and they all worked hard on them. The village became very prosperous and many new houses were built. Everyone was amazed when they remembered that all this wealth came from the piece of straw that Shobei had picked up.

Shobei became the most important man in the village and everyone respected him greatly. And for as long as he lived, they all addressed him as "Mr. Lucky Straw."

Why the Jellyfish Has No Bones

Long ago all the sea creatures lived happily in the palace of the Dragon King, deep at the bottom of the sea—well, almost all of them. The octopus, who was the palace doctor, disliked the jellyfish immensely. In those days, the jellyfish still had bones like all the other creatures.

One day the daughter of the Dragon King became sick. The octopus came to see her and said she would die unless she took a medicine made from the liver of a monkey. "The jellyfish is a good swimmer," said the octopus to the king, "so why not send him to find a monkey's liver?"

And so the king called the jellyfish and sent him on the important errand. But finding a monkey's liver wasn't easy. Even finding a monkey was difficult. The jellyfish swam and swam for days and finally, near a little island, he found a monkey who had fallen in the sea.

"Help, help!" called out the monkey, who couldn't swim.

"I'll help you," said the jellyfish, "But in return you must promise to give me your liver so that we can make a medicine for the Dragon King's daughter." The monkey promised, so the jellyfish carried him on his back and went swimming away toward the palace.

The monkey had been willing to promise anything while he was drowning, but now that he was safe he began to think about his promise. The more he thought, the less he liked the idea of giving up his liver, even for the Dragon King's daughter. No, he decided, he didn't like it one little bit. Being a very clever monkey, he said, "Wait, wait! I just remembered that I left my liver hanging on a tree branch back on the island. Take me back there and I'll get it for you."

So the jellyfish returned to the island. The monkey climbed up a tall tree and then called out to the jellyfish, "Thank you very much for saving me! I can't find my liver anywhere, but I'll just stay here, thank you!"

The jellyfish realized that he had been tricked, but there was nothing he could do about it. He swam slowly back to the palace at the bottom of the sea and told the Dragon King what had happened. The king was very angry.

"Let me and the other fish beat this no-good fellow for you," said the wicked octopus to the king.

"All right, beat him hard," said the king.

So they beat the jellyfish until all his bones were broken. He cried and cried, and the octopus laughed and laughed.

Just then the princess came running in. "Look!" she cried, "I'm not sick at all. I just had a little stomach-ache."

The Dragon King realized that the octopus had lied to them so that he could get even with his enemy, the jellyfish. The king became so furious that he sent the octopus away from the palace forever and made the jellyfish his favorite. So this is why the octopus now lives alone, scorned and feared by all who live in the sea. And this is why, even though he still has no bones and can no longer swim quickly, the jellyfish is never bothered by the other creatures of the sea.

The Old Man Who Made Trees Blossom

Once upon a time there was a very kind old man and his wife who lived in a small village in Japan. Next door to them lived a very mean old man and his wife. The kind old couple had a little white dog named Shiro. They loved Shiro very much and always gave him good things to eat. But the mean old man hated dogs, and every time he saw Shiro he would throw stones at him.

One day Shiro was barking loudly in the yard. The kind old man went out to see what was the matter. Shiro kept barking and barking and began digging in the ground. "Oh, do you want me to help you dig?" asked the old man. He brought a spade and began digging. Suddenly his spade hit something hard. He dug deeper and found a small pot of gold buried in the earth! The kind old man took it into his house and thanked Shiro for leading him to the gold.

Now the mean old man and his wife had been spying on their neighbor and had seen all this. They wanted some gold for themselves. So the next day the mean old man asked if he could borrow Shiro for a while. "Why, of course you may borrow Shiro, if he can be of any help to you," said the kind old man.

The mean old man took Shiro out to his field. "Now find me some gold too," he ordered the dog, "or I'll beat you." So Shiro began digging at a spot on the ground. The mean old man tied Shiro to a tree and

began digging for himself. But all he found was some terrible-smelling garbage! This made him so angry that he hit Shiro on the head with his spade, and killed him.

The kind old man and his wife were very sad about Shiro. They buried him in their field and planted a pine tree over his grave. And every day they went to Shiro's grave and watered the pine tree lovingly.

The tree began to grow very quickly, and in only a short time it became very big. The kind old woman said, "Remember how Shiro used to love to eat rice cakes? Let's cut down the tree and make a mortar from its trunk. Then with the mortar we'll make some rice cakes in memory of Shiro." So the kind old man cut down the tree and made a mortar. He filled it full of steamed rice and began pounding it to make rice cakes. But no sooner had he begun pounding than all the rice turned into gold! Now the kind old man and his wife were richer than ever.

The mean old man and his wife had been peeping through the window and had seen the rice turn to gold. They wanted some gold for themselves. So the next day the mean old man asked if he could borrow the mortar. "Why, of course you may borrow it," said the kind old man.

The mean old man took the mortar home and filled it full of steamed rice. "Now watch," he said to his wife. "When I begin pounding this rice, it will turn into gold." But when he began pounding, the rice turned instead into terrible-smelling garbage! This made him so angry that he chopped the mortar up and burned the pieces in his fireplace.

When the kind old man went to get his mortar back, it was burned to ashes. He was very sad because the mortar had reminded him of Shiro. So he asked for some of the ashes and took them home with him.

It was the middle of winter and all the trees were bare. The kind old man decided to scatter some of the ashes in his garden. When he did this, all the cherry trees in the garden suddenly began to bloom. Everybody came to see this wonderful sight, and even the prince who lived in a nearby castle heard about it.

Now the prince had a cherry tree that he loved very much. Each year he could hardly wait for spring to come so that he could see its beautiful cherry blossoms. But when spring had come that year he discovered that the tree was dead and he was very sad. Now he sent for the kind old man and asked him to bring his tree back to life.

The old man took some of the ashes and climbed up the tree. Then he threw the ashes up into the dead branches, and before they knew it, the whole tree was covered with the most beautiful cherry blossoms that they had ever seen.

The prince was very pleased. He gave the kind old couple a great box of gold and many presents. Best of all, he gave the old man a new title, "Sir Old-Man-Who-Makes-Trees-Blossom."

Sir Old-Man-Who-Makes-Trees-Blossom and his wife were now very rich, and they lived very happily for many more years.

The Crab and the Monkey

Once a crab and a monkey went for a walk together. Along the way the monkey found a persimmon seed, and the crab found a rice ball. The monkey wanted the crab's rice ball, and being a very clever talker, he finally persuaded the crab to trade the rice ball for the persimmon seed. The monkey quickly ate the rice ball.

The crab couldn't eat the persimmon seed, but he took it home and planted it in his garden, where it began to grow. Because the crab watered it carefully every day, it grew and grew.

The tiny seed finally became a big tree, and one autumn day the crab saw that it was full of beautiful persimmons. The crab wanted very much to eat the persimmons, but no matter how hard he tried, he couldn't climb the tree. So he asked his friend the monkey to pick the persimmons for him.

Now, the monkey loved persimmons even more than rice balls, and once he was up the tree he began eating all the ripe persimmons, and the only ones he threw down to the crab were hard and unripe. One of them hit the crab on the head and hurt him badly.

The crab was angry and asked three of his friends, a mortar and a hornet and a chestnut, to help him punish the monkey. So the three friends hid themselves around the crab's house one day, and the crab invited the monkey to come to tea.

When the monkey arrived he was given a seat by the fireplace. The chestnut was hiding in the ashes roasting himself, and suddenly he burst out of the fireplace and burned the monkey on his neck. The monkey screamed with pain and jumped up.

In an instant the hornet flew down and stung the monkey with his tail. The monkey tried to run away, but the mortar was hiding above the door and fell down with a thud on the monkey, hurting his back.

The monkey saw there was no escape. He bowed down to the crab and his three friends and said, "I did a bad thing when I ate the Crab's delicious persimmons and threw the unripe ones to him. I promise never to do such a bad thing again. Please forgive me!"

The crab accepted the monkey's apology, and they became friends again. The monkey learned his lesson and never again cheated anyone.

The Ogre and the Rooster

There once was a mountain so high and steep that it seemed to touch the sky. On top of this mountain lived a terrible ogre. He had red skin and a single horn growing out of his head, and he was always doing wicked things to the village people at the foot of the mountain.

One morning the farmers of the village who worked at the foot of the mountain went to their fields and saw their vegetables ruined. Someone had pulled them all up and had trampled on them until there was not a single good one left.

They wondered who could have done such a thing, then saw the ogre's footprints all over the ground.

This made the farmers angry. They were tired of the ogre's tricks, and when they looked at all the ruined vegetables they became angrier. They pointed up at the mountain and cried, "Oh, you wicked ogre! Why don't you quit doing these wicked things?"

The ogre looked down at them from the top of the mountain and answered in a terrible voice, "You must give me a human every day for my supper. Then I'll stop bothering you!"

The farmers had never heard such a request. They shook their tools at the ogre and shouted back, "Who do you think you are, wanting to eat a human every day?"

"I'm the ogre-est ogre in the land," the ogre roared back. "That's who I am! There's absolutely nothing I can't do! Ha, ha, ha!" The ogre's voice echoed loudly through the mountains and made all the trees bend and sway.

"All right then," yelled back the farmers. "Let's see how great you really are! If you can build a stone stairway with a hundred steps in one night, from our fields all the way to the top of the mountain, then we'll do whatever you want."

"Why, I can do that!" the ogre replied. "And if I haven't finished the stairway before the first rooster crows tomorrow morning, then I promise to go away and to never bother you again."

As soon as it grew dark, the ogre crept into the village and put a straw hood over the head of every single rooster so it wouldn't see the sun rising. Then the ogre thought to himself, "Now I'll build that stairway!" And he set to work, building the stairway up the mountain.

The ogre worked so hard and so quickly that he already had ninety-nine steps in place when the sun began to rise in the east. But he only smiled to himself, thinking that the roosters wouldn't be able to crow and that he still had plenty of time to put the last step in place.

But a kind fairy also lived on the mountain. The fairy had been watching the ogre and had seen the mean trick he was playing. So while the ogre was going down the stairway for the last stone, the fairy flew down and took the straw hood off the head of one of the roosters.

The rooster saw the sun rising and crowed loudly, "ko-ke-kok-ko!" This woke up all the other roosters, and they all began to crow.

The ogre was surprised to hear this. "I've lost!" he cried. "And there was just one more step to go." But even ogres must keep their promises, so he stroked his horn very sadly and went far away into the mountains.

No one ever saw the ogre again and the farmers lived very happily at the foot of the mountain. They finished the stairway up the mountain and often climbed it on summer evenings to enjoy the wonderful view.

The Rabbit Who Crossed the Sea

Once there was a white rabbit who wanted to cross the sea. Across the waves he could see a beautiful island and he wanted very badly to go there. But the rabbit couldn't swim and there were no boats around. Then he had an idea.

He called to a shark in the sea and said, "Oh, Mr. Shark, which one of us has the most friends, you or I?"

"I'm sure I have the most friends," said the shark.

"Well, let's count them to make sure," said the rabbit. "Why don't you

have all your friends line up in the sea between here and that island? Then I can count them."

So all the sharks lined up in the sea, and the rabbit went hopping from the back of one shark to the next, counting, "One, two, three, four, five . . ." Finally he reached the island.

Then he turned to the sharks and said, "Ha, ha, you dumb sharks! I certainly fooled you. I got you to make a bridge for me, without you knowing about it."

The sharks became very angry. One of them reached up with his sharp teeth and bit off a piece of the rabbit's fur.

"Oh, that hurts!" cried the rabbit and he began weeping.

Just then the king of the island came by. He asked the rabbit what was the matter, and when he had heard the rabbit's story, he said, "You mustn't ever fool others and tell lies again. If you promise to be good, I'll tell you how you can get your fur back."

"Oh, I promise, I promise," said the rabbit.

So the king gathered some bulrushes and made a nest with them. "Now you sleep here in this nest of bulrushes all night," said the king, "and your fur will grow back."

The rabbit did as he was told. The next morning he went to the king and said, "Thank you very, very much. My fur grew back and I'm well again. Thank you, thank you, thank you."

Then the rabbit went hopping off along the seashore, dancing and singing. He never tried to fool anyone again.

The Grateful Statues

Once upon a time there lived a kind old couple in a village in Japan. They were very poor and spent every day weaving hats out of straw. Whenever they finished a number of hats, the old man would take them to the nearest town to sell.

One day the old man said to the old woman, "It will be New Year's Day in two days. How I wish we had some rice cakes to eat then! Even one or two little cakes would be enough. Without rice cakes we won't be able to celebrate the new year."

"Well, then," said the old woman, "after you've sold these hats we're making, buy some rice cakes for New Year's Day."

So early the next morning the old man took the five new hats that they had made and went to town to sell them. But when he got to town he was unable to sell a single hat. And to make things worse, it began to snow very heavily.

The old man felt very sad as he trudged wearily home with his hats. He was walking down a lonesome mountain trail when he suddenly came upon a row of six stone statues of Jizo, the protector of children, all covered in thick snow.

"My, my! Now isn't this a pity," said the old man. "These are only stone statues of Jizo, but even so, just think how cold they must be, standing here in the snow."

"I know what I'll do!" said the old man to himself. He unfastened the five new hats from his back and began tying them, one by one, onto the heads of the statues.

When he came to the last statue he suddenly realized that all the new hats had been used. "Oh, my!" he said, "I don't have enough hats." But then he remembered his own scarf. So he took it off his head and tied it on the head of the last statue. Then he went on his way home.

When he got home the old woman was waiting for him by the fire. She took one look at him and cried, "You must be frozen half to death! Quick, come sit by the fire. What did you do with your scarf?"

The old man shook the snow out of his hair and came to the fire. He told the old woman how he had given all the new hats as well as his own scarf to the six Jizo statues. He also said he was sorry that he hadn't been able to bring home any rice cakes.

"That was a very kind thing you did for the statues," said the old woman. She was very proud of the old man and said, "It's better to do a kind thing like that than to have all the rice cakes in the world. We'll get along without any rice cakes for New Year's Day."

Since it was already late at night, the old man and woman soon went to bed.

Just before dawn, while they were still asleep, a very wonderful thing happened. Suddenly there was the sound of voices in the distance, singing:

"A kind old man walking in the snow,
Gave all his hats to the stone Jizo,
So we bring him gifts with a yo-heave-ho!"

The voices came nearer and nearer, and then the sound of footsteps could be heard in the snow.

The footsteps came right up to the house where the old man and woman were sleeping. And then all at once there was a great noise, as though something heavy had been put down just in front of the house.

The old couple jumped out of bed and ran to the door. When they opened it, what do you suppose they found?

Placed very neatly in front of the house was the biggest and most beautiful rice cake the old couple had ever seen.